The Blacken Forest Series

By Christopher Hicks

"There is no escaping the endless nightmare, which twists through you like the worm that feasts on your soul. Beg for mercy you say? Thou worm has no mercy. Lest ye awake from this nightmare, others will call reality." – The Worm

About the book

The Blacken Forest is a short story series written by author Christopher Hicks. The story covers many different encounters of a fantasy-horror based forest with creatures in it by people. Some say the forest cleanses you of your sins, while others wander in the forest for all eternity. Longing for freedom of the reality they once knew. Can you escape the forest?

 ISBN #: 978-1-304-96784-8

Table of Contents

The Blacken Forest

Tis' the night hour that he awoken from the horrors of the nightmares with-in. He searched for answers remembering the words of the worm who spoke so softly to his open soul. *"There is no escaping the endless nightmare that twists through you like the worm that feasts on your soul. Beg for mercy you say? Thou worm has no mercy. Lest ye awake from the nightmare, others call reality."* The words haunted his poor soul, as the aches of the worms words taunted him. He began to walk, constant yet weary. To the door he stood, looking at it with wonder.

Opening the door he saw the forest that which he never seen before. The worm stood tall before him and spoke *"The darkest hour in which one who awaits the beast of the blacken forests. He who says thine name be spoken loudly. The skulls that hold the treasures of the earth be blessed and still upon you. Holden deeper to the truths of the wisdom of the beast."*

The man stood there before the worm, looking at the forest which lays behind him. *"Thou worm, who speaks so gently upon thy beast of this forest. Where art thou who finds this beast?"* The worm watched the man with his six eyes, not saying anything the worm then lead him into the blacken forest. The journey's felt so long, the trees stood tall nearly reaching the heavens above. The worm stopped before a cave in which skulls surrounded and flames reach high as Hades.

The worm turned around to the man and spoke *"Upon your journey thy beast lies with-in the cave you so see. Life is but chances young human, yours begun here with the beast that thou remembers your wrong deeds."* The man stood there scared looking towards the cave. He walks slowly and cautiously to the caves entrance., looking upon the skulls he panics looking back toward the worm *"Why must thou enter such darkness and death, O worm of six eyes and wisdom?"* The worm looks back towards the man saying *"Thou must face your worse and most repressed fears entering the cave. Death is the only way out of here if thou doesn't make the right choices."*

The man stood even more scared looking back towards the eternal dark cave. The flames outside rose taller as he ran into the cave panting hard. He said out loudly *"Thou have entered the darken cave, told by the six eyed worm of wisdom. What must thou do now?"* A roar came from the deepest parts of the cave as the room brightened by the creature's eyes.

"Human you've entered my domain in searches of truth and justice?" The creature says in a

deep voice shaking the cave walls. *"Thou great creature, I know nothing of what is to happen. Thou six eyed worm spoke of you as the blacken beast."* The man said as he walked backwards pushing up against the wall where the entrance once was. The beast said to the man *"Thou wishes for redemption and truth! Ye knows thou wrongs in the past and yet thou does nothing? I offer you nothing human. But the journey's you must conquer to know your faults."*

The entrance reappears as the beast vanished into the darkness of the eternal caves. The man then walked back out approaching the six eyed worm. The worm then said *"Thou knows ye journey and I will take the through it."* He began to walk with the worm as he then came upon a hill, surrounded by weeping willow trees. The worm spoke *"Your next journey lies ahead here young human."*

He looked upon the hill seeing a giant creature standing in the dark. The hill then shined upon the moons light, bursting through the weeping willows. He saw the creature which had three heads of a black widow spider. *"So ye are the one who seeks the justice of the blacken forest?"* The spider said upon the man. *"Who art thee?"* The man said sternly to the spider creature. *"I am Makatorus, the bringer of justice through the lies you so blinded yourself by. You seek thee now you know thee."*

He stood before the giant creature saying *"What have I done, O' creature? I know nothing of my wrongs."* The spider yelled back towards the man *"You know what thou has done! An' thou wilt not go unpunished! Thou must fight thee with the sword of honesty which rests before thee."* The man grabbed the sword as the creature landed before him. *"Ye must fight! Do it now or thou dies before the lies you so blinded yourself by!"* The spider said to the man preparing to attack him with his six fangs.

The man rushed over around the spider as he attempts to stab the creature in the back. The spider smacked the man hitting him off the hill. *"Thou six eyed worm, how do I defeat thy creature?"* He spoke to the worm. The worm replied *"Remember the lies whom you blinded yourself by to cover the fact you're guilty. The spider feeds off the lies of injustice."* The man began to think dodging the spider's blunt attacks. The spider spoke *Thou proves yourself weak before me! This dishonor will be punished!"* The man raced through his memories locked deep with-in his mind, then in the sudden moment he began to uncover the truths. *"I murdered someone!"* He yelled before the spider. The spider then stopped the attacks and looked before the man. *"Thou realized thou wrongness through the fear of death, for this you've conquered me. But now must see the gentle one for the freedom to the beast again."*

The spider said then vanishing into the darkness as the moon became covered in the cloudy skies.

"Now thou must go to the next part of your journey. I shalt lead ye to it, but this time your test is of the mind." The worm said to the man leading him deeper into the forest. The man said to the worm *"I remember the crimes I have committed, I murdered someone. How must thou be forgiven, O' sixed eyed worm?"* The worm said nothing to the man as they reached a tall tree. The worm the said *"Your journey lies up there in the tree young human."*

He looked towards the tree then back towards the worm *But thou worm I fear the heights of the tree."* The worm replied gently *Haven't thou learned that fear is the key to overcoming? You must go upon this tree or suffer the endless death."* The man then stood still, looking the tree up and down. He then reached his arm out and began to climb the tall tree, through hours of climbing his arms cramped and he nearly fell from the tree. Gasping for air he reattached himself to the tree.

Looking up he then saw a light coming from a hole in the tree. Rushing up further to the light, he then fell landing on a branch. He yelled out in pain but not giving up on reaching his destination. He then reached the bright light which came from the hole in the tree. He entered it and spoke *"I am here! What must thou do now?"*

A owl walked out before the man his four wings wrapped around the man holding him in the air. *"Human you awoke thee. I am Alfarus, the keeper of judgment of the beast of the blacken forest."* The man gasped trying to free himself. He looked the owl in the eyes saying *"I come before ye four winged one in the hopes of freedom. I realize my crimes I have committed before thee and ask for forgiveness!"*

The owl looked before the man, then laughing saying *“Small human I give no forgiveness. But I show you the errors of your ways. You have seen your wrong doings for now I must assure you that you know it to be true.”* The owl then peaked the man, causing him to bleed. He then went into a state of trance seeing the people he had murdered in the past. Gasping as he fell from the owls clutches, he looked before the owl *“I have done thou most terrible of crimes, O’ four winged one, how must I be forgiven?”* The owl replied *Forgiveness comes from the one who realizes his own faults. You must do this by returning to the beast of the blacken forest.*

Giving your vary words of knowing your wrongness."

The man then began to climb back down the tree. Reaching the ground he then looked before the worm. *"It is time you reacquaint yourself with thou beast. This wilt be your final journey."* The worm spoke to the man leading him back towards the cave. The flames this time were dim. He walked into the cave shouting for the beast. The cave then lit up by the beasts eyes which shined blue. *Human of lies, you have journeyed through the blacken forest. Knowing your deeds cannot go unpunished. Ye must be punished for the crimes you committed in both our realm and the earth. You have succeeded human, in your punishments here. Your fears of spiders, heights and darkness overcame by the will to live and know. I offer you to reality of this nightmare which will return if you fail to come to terms with the crimes. Be thou well human, for now your journey here ends."* The cave darkened as the man woke from the dream.

He then walked cautiously to the door, opening it seeing the road and neighboring houses.

Hearing the words the beast spoke to him over and over *"Knowing your deeds cannot go unpunished. Ye must be punished for the crimes you committed in both our realm and the earth."* The man then walked to the city jail house admitting to the murders of the people he killed so long ago.

"Know this humans. Even though your deeds may seem to go unpunished for so long in thee realm of the humans. We await in the deepest crevices of your mind. Awaiting to show you the

errors of your ways." –Quote the beast of the blacken forest.

The Fallen: The Blacken Forest II

May 15th, 1987

Upon a night one late spring a man prepared for bed. Laughing at the fact of his wealth from robbing a bank and the police had no lead on the criminal. He slept soundly to the excitement of over one million dollars. But the beauty of the dreams began to become nightmarish. He toss and turned to the dreams which haunted him. Appearing then before the worm he sought the escape out, ignoring the words of the creature whom stood before him. *"You ignore the words of wisdom that thou give thee? This shalt be your fate of crossing the Blacken Forest alone. Thou beast lies north of you."* The worm had said to the man, then in an instant vanishing into the darkness of the forest.

The man struggled finding a way out of the forest. Running through endless tress which stood nearly tall as he. Running he stumbled upon a rock which laid in-front of the cave. The cave which had skulls of the victims of the past with treasures in them. The flames roared at the man as he stepped back from the darken pit of the inferno that he must enter.

Continuing to run the opposite way from the cave, he realized no matter the distance he ran he would end up back at the cave. Running continuously in circles he began to wear out. Then plotting in his mind to enter or continue the never ending dream of escape. After countless hours that passed by, the man decided to give up on running and to enter the darken cave.

He slowly walked in, feeling out the are slowly. The entrance vanished placing him into a panic as he ran through the cave. He then came to a complete stop and roars echoed the cave walls, rumbling the old cave.

The man stood there paralyzed in fear. A creature with eyes of red came to him, the cave became not so dark as the giant creature was before the man. *"Who are you?"* The man asked the creature with a stutter as he backtracked away from the beast. *"I am thou beast which you seek. I am the one who will deliver you the fate of the Blacken Forest."* The beast replied looking before the man.

The man looked before the beast, still paralyzed in fear. He worked up the courage to then respond *"What is this? Am I dreaming? Why am I here?"* The beast looked at the man replying *"Ye of so many questions, know the answers. You know your crimes yet you continue to laugh in the faces of others. Through this, your journeys through the forest will be hard. A dream thou ask? Hardly not the reality you believe is so."* The man then looked down, smiling and laughing before the beast.

"You expect me to apologize for what I did? I shall do no such thing." The man said to the beast laughing at it. The beast let out a loud roar before the man *"You dare mock what I am giving you? For this your journey's will be even harder."* The cave darkened as the entrance reappeared before the man.

Walking out of the cave he noticed the worm *"You're back?"* The man said sarcastically towards the worm. The worms eyes followed the man as he walked towards the worm. *"Your foolishness will not grant you the escape you so desire. Thou must follow me through the forest. This is thou last chance."* The man laughed and replied *"Fine. But this is all non-sense to me."* The worm then lead him into the forest. What seemed like hours of walking they arrived to a old worn down house. The house was made from the trees and leaves surrounding it. There seemed to be no door yet the man then hesitated from entering.

A creature walked out of the house, it had the head of a ant. It looked before the man *"You're the new one to our forest?"* The creature said.

The man looked at the creature and replied *"What are you?"* The creature laughed at the man *"I knew you would ask me this. I am Le'rah. The creature of ego."* The man then hesitated to speak. He looked at the ground beneath him and then spoke to the creature *"Ego?"* Le'rah looked before the man silent and not saying a word. The trees came to life in an instant and grabbed the man with vines. *"Your egotistical ways will not get you far here. I offer you to admit you're wrong. Or you will remind here forever, hanging from the trees in your lifeless corpse."*

The man then had a sudden change of attitude, he looked before the worm *"Help me!"* He yelled echoing throughout the forest. The worm remained silent. The man struggled in the vines the trees held him up on. He then looked back towards Le'rah *"I am egotistical! There I admitted it! Now let me down!"* He yelled loudly. The vines then dropped him as he landed before the ant creature.

"Through the fears you have of being retrained, you've admitted your ignorance before me." The creature said then vanishing into the darkness of

the house. The man walked over to the worm and they proceeded into the forest. *How much more of this do I need to do?* He asked the worm in a more pleasant voice. The worm still leading the way further into the forest replied to the man *"Till you have learned that thou crimes do not go unpunished. You must realize that laughing in others pains and your selfish greed is the error of your existence."*

The man continued walking with the worm remaining silent till they had reached a bolder that was taller than himself and the worm. He awaiting knowing another creature was to come. The bolder cracked open as a giant creature came out of it. The creature had three heads, one of a ram, bull and goat. It had long legs of a goat and six arms reaching out to the skies above. He backed up running into the worm *Oh my god!"* The man said screaming.

The creature looked down before him *"There is no god here for you. Only us who dwell in the darkness of the Blacken Forest."* The man asked the creature *"Who are you and what are you?"* The creature snarled as it grabbed a skull crushing it *"I have many names but you may call me Daeus."* The creature then walked towards the man as the man backed up from the creature. *"Are you going to kill me?"* The man asked. *"That is clearly up to you."* The creature replied.

The man looked before the creature. The creature suddenly grabbed the man holding him many miles above the forest. He screamed and cried, twitching in the clutches of the giant creature. *"Alright! I admit I was wrong, let me go!"* The creature laughed from its three heads, then saying *"You're foolish to think I would believe such lies."*

The man then grew angry towards the creature, spitting in its faces. The creature's heads growled ripping the man in half, his guts covered the trees and the grown below. The creature through the ripped corpse into the forest. The creatures below who had heads of vultures tore the guts and ripped the flesh of the man.

Devouring his entire body in minutes. Through the feces of the bird creatures the man was then reborn to suffer the same fate for all eternity. He ran through the forest never finding a way out, running into the giant creature to suffer the same fate again. The vulture creatures tore out for his hanging flesh devouring him over and over into a bottomless pit of the inferno.

The Blacken Forest III: Wrath of The Fallen King

Once upon the hour of power the forest represented the truth and the greatness. But before the times of the Worm and the beast ruled the beetle king Masaru. He was the true evil of evils and had no mercy for the foolishness of the humans who entered the forest.

But the great beetle king fell before the beast and his creatures. Masaru and his three creatures; Tenarji, the three headed serpent,

Valagora, the three eyed toad and Anar, the beautiful queen of light who had the head of an eagle and the body of a human women. Anar was said to be the mother of the beast.

The great Masaru swore upon his fall that he would rise once again and take the Blacken Forest back to his control. This is the story of the wrath of the beetle king.

It was the time I returned to the forest I once was, that so long ago the worm taught me the meanings of life and death. The knowledge of the blacken forest was upon me. I drifted to a place where the illusions of reality and the truth of dreams would keep me safe. That I searched for guidance of the worm and the creatures of the blackened forest.

I then opened my eyes seeing the forest clearly. The fires from the distant cave lightened the way. Where I then seen the Book of Adenio. I then read from the passages of the worm *"Lord of the journey's, come before me in the will of the forest. I call to you under the twelve moons in the sky. Worm be before thy!"*

The worm appeared before me in shock of seeing me return to the forest I escaped from long ago. I told the worm that I needed his guidance and the worm lead me to the cave where I saw the beast's eyes *"Thou O' beast. I need thou guidance."* The beast listened to me as the cave begun to shake. The beast vanished into the darkness as I walked outside seeing the ground shake, the winds picked up blowing the flames out making the trees fall.

I looked before the worm *"What is happening?"* The worm looked before me and said *"Thou human you have arrived into danger. The fallen king has returned in search of vengeance. You must return back to your plane. The book shalt have a passage to create a doorway to your home."* I looked before the worm and replied *"I shalt not leave. I will pay my owes in helping you."* The worm looked at me like I was foolish yet brave and accepted my proposal.

The worm lead me through the forest as I seen the trees destroyed and the skies were fire red. I seen from a distance the bright fires which lit up the remaining forest trees. We then stopped as the other creatures of the beast stood there. They looked before me and looked back. I seen more creatures standing beside a large bolder with flames around it. The beetle headed creature stood on the bolder speaking to them. I looked before the worm *"That is the fallen king. His creatures look powerful. How can we defeat them?"*

The worm responded *"We engage in battle against the fallen king."* The worm lead the creatures of the beast into the area which the fallen king is in. The fallen king roared sending his creatures at them. I remained in the shadows feeling useless.

I then seen the creatures of the fallen king defeating the beasts creatures. I grabbed a sword flying out into the battle ground. The creatures tossed, thrown and tore me up. Nearly dead laying on the ground, Alfarus the great four winged owl picked me up.

He flew me to safety by the cave where the beast was *"Stay here human. Read the passage of the fallen one. Send Masaru back to the underforest."* Alfarus said flying back to the battle. I picked the book up.

Trying to read the foreign language it had troubled me to read a language I have never seen nor spoken. I could hear the cries of the creatures as the fallen king was approaching victory. I ran fast through the forest to the battle chanting out the words of the passage. The ground shook, nearly knocking me off my balance.

The fallen king seen me chanting as he flew in the air, his ten wings took the night sky as he landed before me. His wings had pointy ends which were sharper than a katana. I kept chanting as the fallen king said to me *"Thou worthless human dares to speak the ancient words of the Forest? Ye believes thou can send me back? I shalt smite thee and send you to the underforest."* The fallen king sent his wing into my chest shoving me back into a tree. The book fell from my hands as I grinned at the fallen king saying *"I.. I finished the passage."*

The fallen king screamed in anger as a flash of lightning struck him and his creatures sending them back to the underforest. The worm rushed to me as I laid there dying. *"Bravery makes you strong. This thou human makes you one of us."* The worm had Alfarus fly me to the cave where the beast looked before me in respect. *"Thou act of courage will go rewarded. As your human body dies, you shalt live forever in the forest. I name you Jaruse. Ye shall have the head of a lion, four white wings and claws of a hawk. Jaruse the brave one."*

My eyes closed as I then awoke in the cave. I looked at my claws seeing that I was now a creature of the beast. The Forest, the beast, the honor rewarded me with the potential to helping others and growing the Blacken Forest.

No act goes unpunished nor unrewarded. Thus I learned this on my new journey into the Blacken Forest. I was born Earl Scott III, a human and I was reborn as Jaruse, a creature of bravery.

Into the mind of The Blacken Forest

The creatures and the purpose of the forest are beyond what words can represent. The reasons and stories of how the creatures of The Blacken Forest came to be.

Makatorus (Maa-ka-torous) The Bringer of Justice

Many years ago a young women was taunted by a dark beast. Her name was Martha Lee Townsend she was a peasant girl from the

United Kingdom in the late 1600's. Her dreams were recorded by her father James R. Townsend as a worm known as the 'Six Eyed Worm'. The worm lead her to a creature known as the beast. This creature brought her through a forest of illusions where she faced her worse fears. She died in the early 1700's where she became Makatorus. The beast sought her fears, pains and desires to be that of Justice of the three headed spider.

Alfarus (Al-far-ous) The Keeper of Judgment

Long after the death of Martha Lee Townsend a young man from a small growing country of America in the 1750's was recorded by his friend. The man was Richard Tyler who said he was taunted by a beast and a spider. He was a lawyer and used his power to condemn the innocent. He died days after saying this. The beast found his passions to judging others for their wrong doings and gave him the powers of Alfarus, the four winged owl.

The Six Eyed Worm, Guide of the Blacken Forest

The story of the Sixed Eyed Worm comes from an old man who lived by himself in a forest in Ireland back in the 1500's. He secluded himself from the world after his wife and kids died. His kindness though before his seclusion intrigued the beast in making him the guide known as The Six Eyed Worm. His six eyes represents the sight through the Blacken Forest.

Upon a night in the late part of winter the beast visited the old man. The old man only showed kindness and deep sorrow towards the beast. The beast proved him worthy of his act of kindness in helping a child find their way out of a cave off the coast of Ireland. His bravery and kindness brought him to being the Six Eyed Worm.

The Beast; King of the Blacken Forest

The term 'beast' brings up many hysteria in the modern world. The beast is a huge creature whom dwells in a cave in the Blacken Forest.

His knowledge represents the justice found within those who've done wrong doings. The Beast has no creation story for he existed before time and space. His eyes either shine red or blue. Symbolizing the persons wrong doing and if they confessed their crimes or sins. Upon going to the Blacken Forest his eyes would shine red, but when completing the journey if his eyes shined blue lighting up the dark cave symbolizes the overcoming of the crimes committed. The beast symbolically represents purity and justice.

Le'rah (Lee-Rah) The creature of Ego

Le'rah is a tall creature that wears a black robe. Le'rah has the head of a ant which is not small. Le'rah was never human and has existed many years beyond that of humans. He is the teacher of overcoming ego.

Daeus (Day-E-Ous) The giant creature

Daeus is the giant powerful creature of the Blacken Forest. He has the head of a ram, bull and goat. He has long legs of a goat and six arms reaching to the skies. He is also like Le’rah and was never human. He is known to be one of the most powerful creatures of the Forest.

The Vulture Creatures

They dwell in the lower half of the Forest, they're violent and rarely have contact with other creatures. They're known to be pets of Daeus. They feast upon those who fail to see what the Blacken Forest really is to them.

Masaru (Mah-Sar-U) The Fallen King

Masaru is the original king of the Blacken Forest. He is the brother of the Beast and the son of Anar. He is cruel and violent towards humans. He has the head of a beetle, ten wings with razor sharp edges (mentioned to be sharper than a katana blade). He is taller than any creature but Daeus. He rose up against the Beast again in the third story and fell to the brave human and the creatures of the Beast. His creatures are; Tenarji, the three headed serpent, Valagora, the three eyed toad and Anar the beautiful queen of light who had the head of a eagle and the body of a human women. Anar was said to be the mother of the beast as well.

The Book of Adenio

The powerful book written by the Great Ones. There is little known so far of them or the book. It is only mentioned in the third part of The Blacken Forest.

The Blacken Forest

This is a realm where all the creatures dwell in. It is built for the journey's symbolizing a person's fear and the crimes committed on the earth. The tree sizes represent the amount of crimes the person committed. If they're tall it symbolizes the person has committed multiple crimes. Upon entering the forest through the front door of the place the person has fallen asleep in, the Six Eyed Worm would greet them generally with a riddle then speaking to the beast.

The worm would lead the person to the beast where the beast would judge them into going on the journey through the Blacken Forest. Not always will the person meet all the creatures. After speaking to the beast the person would travel through the dangerous forest with the Six Eyed Worm. Conquering fears and challenged created by the creatures would decide the fate of the person. Failure to comply to the challenges would result in being trapped in the underforest for all eternity.

The Underforest

The Underforest was mentioned in the third story. It is like the underworld in popular mythology. But the Underforest represents pure pain and torture. Those who fail their journey's would go here. Also the beetle king and his creatures dwell in the Underforest.

Objective of the story

The story symbolizes that even in life, if you get away with a crime the creatures who dwell in this place would taunt the person in their dreams forcing them to come to terms with their crimes. You cannot get away from the crimes you once/or have committed. Though the story plot changes in the third part, this part shows about the war of the fallen king who rises again to conquer the beast.

"O' Worm, I hail to thee in the darkest hour. The pure terror of the trees which speak to me so softly. Quote me thou worm, giver of life and death." –Christopher Hicks

The Art of Flesh

Thou flesh is the symbol of the power of the hungry creatures whom dwell below. The art of the flesh is the passions of the man who holds the greed as his bearer. The creatures whom dwell in the pits of the mind, devour you to the bone. Let your blood run the courses of a mile that the intestine stretch. Your heart beats constantly to the birds peaking your flesh off, using the bones as jewelry to the beasts with-in.

Your organs bring the gifts in the art. Your soul is the blessings that tops of the master piece of death. Twisting heads to the clock ticking desire. Your time runs shorter and shorter as the shuttering winds freeze the open flesh from your devoured body, that this is our art of flesh.

Blood is the paint of the portrait of desire. Bow not before the creatures who threaten your life, for it is the fear of your lifeless body that feeds the hungry birds. Your eyes bring them joyous laughter as the sight of pain grows in you.

Let this be our art of flesh, the horded desires of the lust with-in you. The creatures eat the pleasure from your pathetic soul. Your pain is their joy and music. Your blood is their desire. Your flesh is their art. Never forget these words young soul. For they await you one dark, dark night. Your heart beat fuels the desire and hunger for the flesh that wraps your empty soulless body.

Mesmerizing Lies

The poem found on in the diary of a man who overcame the ego and fears with-in. Written and created by Christopher Hicks.

A knock, A knock the door I approach

Stepping and tapping the sounds it makes

Tossing and turning the children sleep

Comes a toll the mesmerizing lies

Open, Open the door I do

Seeing the worm, Its eyes so many

Lies and lies the truth I dear

Speaking in riddles, the poem its sweet

Hold my head in palms of hands

Tell, Tell O' worm do tell

"Why, Why man of lie. Do you resist my uttering urge?"

"Quiet!" I say, whispering yet loud

Children do sleep, my house of lies

Keeping, Keeping the secrets I hold

That dear ol'worm speaks truth I fear

Murder, Murder! Rumbles the house

"Oh No!" I say loudly and clear

Mesmerizing lies worm so speaks

Truth I dare run from here

Knocking, Knocking the door bangs hard

Worm O' Worm I saith to thou!

"Keep me away! Keep them away!"

Thee worm! Thee worm! He doesn't respond

That the mesmerizing lies be the truth and bound

I run, I rush, I tumble forth

Before me stands the truth I fear

The life, The life I felt so true

Is but the mesmerizing lies, I lived for you.

About the Author

Christopher Hicks was born in Kansas and currently lives in Southern, Missouri. He has always had a passion for writing. Since a young child, Christopher would write poetry, short stories and into his teens even scripts and lyrics. Christopher enjoys spending his time writing, reading, studying, meditating, cooking, singing and even dancing. He loves his family and earns his talents for writing from his Mother Shelly, who also enjoys poetry, short stories and novels.

Christopher Hicks is an avid reader of popular writers like Stephen King, Anne Rice and old school writers like Edgar Allen Poe and H.P Lovecraft. His passion for horror is inspired mostly on Edgar Allen Poe who he considers one of his literary idols. Christopher plans to work on many new books. From horror to even suspense and drama.

Christopher also spends his time as an animal activist and proud animal lover (specially cats).

List of Books by Christopher Hicks

Book Title	Year	Status	Genre
When Hell Comes	2014	Published	Horror
The Blacken Forest Series	2014	Published	Horror-Fantasy
The Reverence of Isabella Series: From Faith	2015-2016	Coming Soon!	Drama
The Return	2016	Coming Soon!	Horror

www.ingramcontent.com/pod-product-compliance
Ingram Content Group UK Ltd.
Pitfield, Milton Keynes, MK11 3LW, UK
UKHW020235250726
13967UKWH00001B/377

9 781304 967848